The Pyramid Builder and Other Stories

Dr. Arnab Chatterjee

pencil

ISBN 978-93-5883-099-6
© Dr. Arnab Chatterjee 2023

Published in India 2023 by Pencil

A brand of
One Point Six Technologies Pvt. Ltd.
Unit no. 26, Ground Floor, Building A1,
Wadala Truck Terminal Road,
Near Post Office, Antop Hill, Mumbai - 400037
E connect@thepencilapp.com
W www.thepencilapp.com

Author biography

Dr. Arnab Chatterjee is presently an Associate Professor of English at the Department of English, Koneru Lakshmaiah Education Foundation (Deemed to be University), Vaddeshwaram, Vijayawada, Andhra Pradesh; India. He has penned poems, a dystopian novel, short stories, academic books and a volume of critical essays. He is the author of *In Desolate Dwellings, Residence Beneath the Earth*and the long narrative poem *The Wind in the Abyss*, that make up *The Reflections Trilogy*. An alumnus of St. Xavier's College, as well as Presidency College, Kolkata, his name appears in the prestigious *Who's Who of Indian Writers Writing in English*(ISBN: 978-81-260-4812-0), a nation-wide record of writers compiled by The Sahitya Akademi, New Delhi, the National Academy of Letters of India. He has penned over ten volumes of poetry, some of which have been published and others awaiting publication. His hobbies include listening to music, academic research, writing and travelling. *Cranberry Heart*is his latest volume of poems. This is his recent foray into the genre of short stories. He can be contacted at <carnab393@gmail.com> and +91-9330473173. Read his books at <https://www.amazon.in/Arnab-Chatterjee/e/B082RCC25Y/ref=aufs_dp_fta_dsk>

CONTENTS

Preface

These stories have been brimming for quite some time. Honestly, I never thought I would try my hand at prose as I am more comfortable with verse. Till now, I have already penned over 10 volumes of poetry with some already published and well received and others awaiting prospective publishers. Yet, my first short story "Ward no. 17, Paratappur" (that has not been reprinted here and was published in the collection of short stories edited by Dr. Saikat Banerjee, then working in K.N. Modi University, Rajasthan, India, called *The Elusive Genre,* Yking Books, Jaipur, 2016) led me to write more and here are ten additional pieces. The themes are varied. Yet, they seek to present the panorama of existence and how varied and multi-layered human perception is. I hope the readers would like them. I do not fail to say that many of them have their genesis in the situations I have come across all these years.

I thank Pencil Publishers for bringing out this book and the excellent job they are doing to move budding writers to the fore. Thanks are also due to my wife Rinki Chatterjee who once told me to concentrate on short stories as she personally believed they tend to have a wider appeal today than other genres. Thanks are also due to my other well-wishers, especially my family that has sustained faith in me. And lastly, to my dear parents who are no longer alive, but do shower their grace.

Happy reading!

Dr. Arnab Chatterjee

Vaddeshwaram

Vijayawada---522502

Andhra Pradesh

India

+91-9330473173

July 2023

Acknowledgements

To Dr. Jayprakash Jala, Associate Dean (Academics) and Deputy Director, International Relations, Koneru Lakshmaiah Education Foundation (Deemed to be University) for inspiring always.

To my dear wife Rinki Chatterjee for inspiring me to try my hand at prose.

To Dr. Debabrata Hazra, friend, colleague, brother and fellow scholar.

To my dearest Muse who inspired my latest volume of poems.

To Dr. K.V. Divya, HoD, Department of English, Koneru Lakshmaiah Education Foundation (Deemed to be University) for her cooperation and understanding.

To my daughter Celina for making my days with a smile and flying kisses.

To my deceased pet cat 'Buddhimaan' to whom a story is dedicated.

To my pet doggo Bruno who inspires my upcoming book of poetry.

CONTENTS

1. The Cup of Tea

It was Pratap's off day in the school. Usually he had a very tough time during the five days, but on Mondays, he would not stir. Mornings would nevertheless start with his wife screaming for milk, but he would laze and go to the milk parlour not before ten. The rest of the day would be taken by television and newspapers. He was supposed to clean the storeroom today, but he somehow dodged the whole task till twelve. By one, his wife was restless lest the garbage collector find faults and not take the entire bunch of useless reading material that had been lying since they came to this house after Pratap's father's death. It was said to contain his father's diaries that, by now, had accumulated cockroach eggs. "Come next year and the garbage man would not take them", his wife would be quick to point out.

It is difficult to say if it was his love for his wife or her fear that he somehow adjusted himself to the boring task of sorting the diaries that his father had accumulated over the last fifty years. The door of the store room was just four feet by five, and Pratap, after a hearty meal after two thirty, somehow crept inside like a truant boy. Though it was clean, the air was musty, but if one sat cross-legged, things would not be nightmarish. His wife had gone to sleep in the mid-August heat of the afternoon, and so he was left to do whatever he pleased till five, when the maid arrived.

He adjusted his glasses, and started piling diaries one by one. Most of them belonged to the late sixties, with the inscription, "From 12th July 1969 to 17th August 1971" and so on. A quite many had no covers at all. Some had lost most of their pages with only the leather cover left, that would probably fetch a good price. But after a good toil of around an hour or so, his attention was fixed at a queer looking diary that belonged not to his father but his grandfather. The date read "15th September 1945." "Oh, what a find!" he thought. He resumed his cross-legged posture and flipped the pages. Most of them were memoirs. At one point, his gaze was transfixed at the title "Based on a true account: not fiction." The narrative went as follows:

'This was the time when me and my father were looking for a good girl whom I could marry. We had roamed through the length and breadth of the city, but my father would disapprove of any girl who was not fair. Even when he approved, I would balk the blunt nose or those tiny, mouse like eyes that would be more interested in our wealth than our inherent nobility. The match-broker was frustrated. Twenty-five girls had been rejected in a span of just six months.

Then, one fine morning, the broker came with some good news—there was a girl but the family was poor, yet they had a good name. My father was furious, "Every match you bring is good! The last time, the girl whom we went to see forgot to touch my feet, before that, the father was kind enough to ask if I favour the British or the revolutionaries. Of course I favour the latter." But the broker was sure of hitting the bull's eye this time. The father had met her in the market place and was eager to see me. He had a long gash on his face that was due to an old war he had fought with the firinghees[1] near the Afghanistan border. But now, he had accommodated himself to the status of a humble farmer. But since the girl was good, and was touted to be a dish, my father condescended.

We took our car and travelled forty miles off Paratapnagar till we could see nothing but the sugar cane fields. The village wherein the 'dish' lived was called Madanpur: a tiny hamlet of not more than a hundred houses and a marketplace. It was nightfall when we reached. This time I had taken the task of driving the car. When we got off, I took out the little sheet of paper that read the name of the father "Sri Himmat Singh." Just before us was a tea stall. We asked the address, but the man was just happy only to show us the direction; he uttered not a single word. This may have been due to the *paan*he chewed. Meandering the dusty lanes, we came to a silent spot—there stood only a single, near-dilapidated house with the sign "Himmat Singh" on a wooden plank invaded by cobwebs.

My father's anger knew no bounds—had not the match-maker informed beforehand that they were to arrive? After my father thought it beneath his position to knock the dusty door any further, I took the honor and knocked the hell out of the same till an eerie voice responded, "come in…why are you outside?" "Country bumpkins!" my father was about to mutter; he had already said a bit of that when I told him to be quiet. In fact, we ought to be more interested in the mango and not the tree.

Whatever be the sad countenance that the house wore from outside, inside, it was snug, warm and even neat. To our utter surprise, there was not even a single cobweb inside the room, and the tables were clean. Himmat Singh, with a long gash that started from his mouth and traversed like the mighty Ganges till his eyebrow suited his six feet six inches tall stature. Though he was a hardy farmer now, his eyes were warm and even kind-looking. He welcomed us with his old rifle on his shoulder, a habit, that he told us, he could not leave. The only pity was that there were no bullets—ever since he had left the British army, he was given the rifle as a souvenir but not the bullets. After a while, the wife appeared. She looked a traditional housewife, with the only difference that she wore no jewellery. That was strange. You receive your would-be son-in-law, and you wear none! It was not that Himmat Singh was in straitened financial circumstances. The pension from the army would never stop presumably, and then he farmed wheat and indigo alternately that would have fetched him a good price.

My father whispered in my ears to ask him why there was such a difference between the exterior of his house and the well-kempt interior. But since we were still guests and the girl was yet to be seen, I desisted. On the table were seen cups of tea, steaming hot, that may have been waiting for us before we entered. Again something fishy—why would the girl not do the honor of serving us snacks and tea?

Himmat Singh was least concerned with my father's affiliation with the British or the revolutionaries, though he had ample reasons to ask. I was getting desperate to see the 'dish', but there was no sign even after an hour. Himmat Singh talked only when he had to, and his eyes were still warm and kind.

All of a sudden, we were petrified by the muffled sound of the girl. The mother rushed. There was something special about the noise—as if someone was choked and was in great pain. My father enquired, and Himmat Singh told us that as the girl wore no clothes at home, and only preferred to do so when outside, her mother had to perforce her! This remark simply plucked out our ear drums. So the girl remained nude at home, and the match maker had decided to slaughter me here!? My father was fuming. After around fifteen minutes, the mother came out with great perspiration and insisted us to finish our tea. My father just wanted to hurl abuses, and I wanted to get out of there.

By now the girl had come out. I was nearly glued to the chair. What were we looking at? A girl of around twenty, fair, long haired, dressed in a sari that draped her figure that gave it even more grace and sustenance. She had dark, nice eyes, and her lashes were prominent. Long nails covered with paint, she smiled as she walked towards my father. She was well endowed, but not to a ridiculous extent. Her forehead was small, but her face was radiant. She wore a bindi on her forehead….the rest defied description. Her youth was a free-flowing river that would nurture millions.

Her name was Malini…the skillful gardener that would look after each and every plant of our family. By this time, my father's anger had somewhat subsided and he was relieved when she touched his feet. She kindly offered me the cup of tea, still hot. But to my astonishment, it would still remain full after I had sipped a full dose. My eyes began to fail me and I could see that my father was also losing consciousness.

When we regained ourselves, we could see daylight had entered the house. To utter dismay, the trio were not to be found. The room was a pigsty. The pan-wallah who had guided us was leaning over. "Oh, sir! Why did you come inside?" "To see the girl," I replied. "What girl? No one lives here for the past ten years. Himmat Singh was killed in a skirmish near the Afghan border; a long gash seven inches wide severed his skull. After his death spread like wild fire, his pension was immediately stopped by the British due to reasons not yet clear. Some say that he betrayed them and joined the revolutionaries secretly running an organization to overthrow the foreign yoke. His wife was left to till the fields; her daughter assisted her for some months. Then, while coming back home, a band of bandits operating under the guidance of the British looted her jewellery, and when they could find nothing on the girl's body, violated her. Their naked bodies were dumped near the pond adjacent to this house. Since then, Himmat Singh's soul has been alluring men to his house on the pretext of seeing his daughter for marriage that he had really planned to do after his return from the frontier."

"And what about the cups of tea that never run out of their contents?", I asked.

"Her daughter hated kitchen chores, and only after much pleading had prepared a cup of tea at the behest of her mother to be given to men who would come to see her within a month or two. It must have been good enough, and the same sits here since ages, still scalding hot."

It seems we were saved only because of my father's affiliation with the revolutionaries.'

2. Early Joys

He was approaching his retirement years and the time would soon come when his second son would be married. He already had a daughter-in-law in the house. His relationship with her was not very cordial, though it was not strained as well. There were some differences between his first son and his wife would partake in that as well as good wives are often wont to. He believed in the old saying that if there are seven utensils together, you ought to expect some noise that is even necessary as well. Wife was long gone and his two sons were still respecting his wishes. But you cannot cling to small shrubs for long if they are fast expanding their tentacles—times would surely come when they would prick and you cannot complain that you once nurtured them and what has come of now!

All in all, the environment and the ambience of Mr. Shrivastava's house was okay; you cannot expect a family picture now-a-days where all are shown with joined hands going to a super market that is often used as a publicity stunt and an ad by emerging shopping malls all over the nation. The new shopping experience of our nation. Joins all in one. All was still okay. Mr. Shrivastava was earning a sum that could not be called measly; he had access to a pension scheme and would get a handsome provident fund post retirement as well. He had no debts and his two sons were well educated and not disobedient. The elder was a computer engineer in a respectable software firm; the younger was a chartered accountant. Mr. Srivastava had dedicated a full thirty eight years in a public sector undertaking and was loved by all, though he had his own share of critics. His only solace when criticized was a sentence that he had read in a book of literary essays when he was a student during his graduation days: "Never mind what a critic says; no statue was ever erected in the honour of a critic."

Whatever be the circumstances in which he was, he would always be lightened up by the figure of hills and ravines. It would be his daily chore to look at those places where he had wandered with his wife post marriage when his first issue was just six years old – old enough to be taken anywhere else. But he was particularly attached to the place where he had spent three years of his life, a tiny town somewhere near the foothills of the Shivaliks called Mirnagar. He was just studying in standard four when his father got transferred to this town lying in the lap of Mother Nature. He would particularly remember the times during recess hours when he would be languidly lying on the soft grass and munching his tiffin. The bell would have rung for the next class but he would linger for more. Then Mr. Ram, his class teacher would be annoyed when he would be late for the Mathematics class. "You are late again! Ok. Tell us all, what is the sum of two.......?" Questions would always come out of Mr. Ram's mouth that would naturally run dry due to his excessive talking. Students would often be bored as whether the number three was an odd or an even number. Mr. Ram would often close his eyes and repeat the same lecture over and over again, and some of the students would manage to sneak out of the class. But Mr. Srivastava would not be one of them. He would then close his eyes as well and think of the tip of those hills where he would one day climb and feel that he has, after all conquered the entire world.

Mr. Shrivastava's reverie was suddenly broken by the entry of his first son Srikant after his posh car had honked before the gate. His obedient wife opened it. It had been a really hard day for him. After having analyzed a computer program that had gone haywire, he had to quickly act as a resource person at an interview that had been hurriedly called to appoint a debugger. Then he was working on a project to design a new program to track malicious mails. His work seemed endless. Mr. Srivastava had been longing to talk to him for quite some time now. But he seldom got a chance. He would be out by nine in the morning, and there were times when he had returned home at two am. There was hardly any time to talk. Since Srikant had become the natural boss of the house (his father had gently allowed this) after his mother's death, it was incumbent for Mr. Srivastava to tell him his inner desires before he slept a sleep that knew no waking.

He somehow tip toed to the room of his son to see what Srikant was doing after an hour had elapsed. He had customarily taken a bath and changed into his clothes that were to be worn after his return from office. His wife was sitting with him. "Should I intrude?" he wondered. But then she was somehow able to watch the prying pose of her father-in-law and nudged her husband. They adjusted themselves.

"Please come in baba", Srikant said.

"I've come at a time not suitable for me. But wanted to talk to you still. We hardly get time."

He pointed his wife to pour some more tea for his father.

Mr. Srivastava decided to come straight to the point. "Actually Sri, there was something that I wanted to tell you. Do you remember Mirnagar?"

"Yes I do. And also that small accident on the ropeway in which a good twelve people were killed. But it was a fine place…" his son's commercial looking eyes suddenly turned nostalgic. "But why Mirnagar after so many years baba?"

"See, I will be retiring the next month. The last time we all took a holiday was a good ten years ago. Then Shalini passed away. You got married. We never had a time. Since Mirnagar was one of the most pleasant periods of my childhood…"

"Not mine!", Srikant was about to erupt. "It was there that we nearly got killed. The authorities had advertised in the newspapers that landslides were imminent, yet we took the ropeway. Remember how we were saved due to the timely snap of the electric connection? Yet how can I forget the scar on my back that still hurts when I try to work for even a hour at a stretch. If they come to know ever…"

"Life will always present its share of obstacles. Yes what happened cannot be changed. What I had come to say that post retirement, I am not in a mood to take a trip to

Hardwar or Rishikesh or somewhere else. I just wish to see the languid clouds of Mirnagar before I die."

"Then you will die once you reach there."

"Situations are different now. And I won't take the aerial ropeway any more. I just wanted to ask you regarding this."

"What's to ask baba. If you have made up your mind, then its ok. But be careful."

Mr. Srivastava was given a grand farewell on the day he retired from his firm. The manager had prepared an eloquent speech in which all the achievements of this person were summed up : how honestly had he worked for the last thirty-eight years and was promoted three times; how he had handled disputes with the then government at the centre when it came to matters of jurisdiction over nation's precious resources and so forth. He was handed over a cheque of a goodly sum and was told to speak on this occasion, to which he consented and did not speak much, as his soul yet yearned for the much-needed trip to that hallowed place.

The day had finally arrived. His eldest son was sure that he would be talking to his father for the last time, as the situation had worsened in that part of the nation after the recent landslides. To this the government has issued a warning that the entry of most of the tourists was restricted (and only the lucky ones could avail the opportunity). Whatever the case, our aged hero was confident of making to the echo hill spot of Mirnagar.

He had finally dressed by five. His train was at night. Since his wife was no more, Srikant had ordered something over home service so that his old father may not go hungry if the train's catering system failed. Mr. Srivastava was lightly dressed and packed, but did not lack the necessaries for trip. He arrived at the station a full hour before the scheduled arrival of the train. A newspaper boy came to him with an evening daily; he bought one and even went to the extent of tipping the chap.

He entered the cheap sleeper class coach with berth 29 as his designated spot. But it was already occupied by some urchins who had neither a ticket for the reserved coach nor a penchant for decent language. The TTE was informed, but he was a dead duck in such matters. He had to share the seat with someone else, who understanding the demeanor of Mr. Srivastava, offered him the same. The urchins kept smoking for the rest of the night and left early in the morning. Till then, he was thoroughly tired because of the precious sleep he had been deprived from.

The train arrived Mirnagar full two hours late. That was the terminal station. He somehow weakly slumped on the berth and adjusted himself before he could get out. A coolie seemed necessary. He had missed the cool air of the window seat that he was supposed to relish, but let that be a bygone issue, he mused.

Outside seemed a long line—the tourist bureau of the area had cordoned off a huge arena due to a landslide the last night. So, he would be missing the echo hill, the deer park and the aerial ropeway. But the lighthouse on the hill that was installed by the new government a few years ago was a thing not be missed. The mega structure was meant to beacon the government vehicles below and to the normal passers-by as well, especially in case of an emergency. He boarded a tempo and was now headed towards that even without considering the need for a quick breakfast.

By the time he had reached the lighthouse, he weakly stood on his legs. The radiant sun of his childhood was before him. Before thumping down on the roadside, he could see her face in the clouds. And that was nice.

3. Dreams

No one knows why we dream at all. Though there are good psychoanalytic theories that say a lot about rapid eye movements and so forth, nothing conclusively has been said about the origin of dreams. Of course, we have Freud, and Jung and Adler who have done some pioneering research on this.

I am not in a mood to advocate theories about dreams; my hectic schedule at my workplace and late hours of work do not permit so. But times come when someone comes to you and tells that s/he has seen a dream and wants to tell you the stuff. And those are the times you cannot refuse.

So, when I reached my flat at around eight in the evening, my little, nine year old daughter crept to me and told about a dream that she dreamt the last night. She had already narrated the same over three times to my wife, and the old, seventy years old maid servant was not around today who has a nasty habit of listening to everything we say to each other. My tea was ready and so was my daughter with a story.

After she narrated the entire story to me, I laughed. It was all about a bird that comes to her bed side and plays with her until she can play no more and tells the bird to retire. The bird, in a fashion reminiscent in some tales, tells her to keep on playing or she will be sucked up by its slender beak. She plays and plays until she can no more. When she is about to be swallowed, my wife well tells her to wake up for a good ten minutes.

My daughter looked at me. She evidently didn't like the grinning. She was of the opinion that her story was not only real, but good as well. Then, she told me to narrate her a story as she had already done one. I thought about one.

I decided to narrate her spooky tale of an old maid looking after a bachelor after it is later discovered that the maid is a witch. This was a real account of a man somewhere living in eastern Africa in the 1800s. I came to know the entire stuff from a book of African tales and folklore. The story went as follows:

'During the time the British were stationed in the Nakuru Rift Valley in Eastern Africa, a young bachelor named Bangwa worked for them. He was a clerk who had, after all, risen to the position of the overseer of the railway project that was going on in the Valley. The workers would strain their muscles day and night and it was Bangwa's job to see to it that the project was completed on time. He would maintain a register that contained the names of nearly all the labourers consigned to this task. He would have a quick meal in the morning and be thick at work until afternoon. Not a single mistake could be committed. He would not be concerned whether it was twelve or one o' clock. Work was all to him. In the morning when he would be leaving his wooden hut, his old maid servant, nearly seventy years old would give him a nutritious meal that he would be ready to eat by noon. The woman had lost her kith and kin a long time ago and had been employed by Bangwa as he too had lost his mother and father the last year after both of them succumbed to a road accident. She was well provided for and had been nice to him after he took her in. But there was just one thing that he could not comprehend. She used to keep a small bunch of hair under her bedside that she would declare was from a lucky woman and acted as a charm for the solution of one's problems. Of course in Africa, voodoo and witch doctors were very common then and you would have a man or a woman keeping various charms in the house that would include, inter alia, owl's beak and toe nails, the hair from a lion's mane and so forth. So, in the beginning Bangwa did not pay much attention to this fact that she kept an assortment of very odd things in the house, but was neat and trim about them. Sometimes, at night he could hear some muffled sounds and knew by heart that they were made by the old woman who must be muttering something in sleep. So, he never made an attempt to know what was what.

One fine morning, when Bangwa had reached the construction site, he was greeted by a fellow worker. He was a rather cheerful guy and would not loose temper as most of the workers did after a day's labour. Bangwa had a good night's sleep as usual. He was more concerned about the murmurings that he had heard the last night. Usually he would not rise quickly and because of the day's hard labour would prefer to sleep as soundly as he could. But the last night, the voices were very unusual. Bangwa kept thinking about the same again and again until it was the turn of his white, European officer to see that something was troubling him. Mr. Richards had a cordial relation with him and despite the colour line would be nice due to his sheer diligence at work. The laboureres were hard at work and it was time for Bangwa to ring the bell for the lunch, something that he didn't. He was awaken by Mr. Richards. Bangwa could understand the blunder that he had committed. In his dictionary, there was no room for such lapses. The cheerful guy who came to him was called Nkuyu who asked him of his troubled countenance. Bangwa, during the lunch time narrated what exactly passed the previous night.

Nkuyu's household had a very long tradition of magic and voodoo. His grandfather who was a well-respected voodoo specialist had the reputation of even curing near-dead people. Nkuyu told after much deliberation that he be allowed into his boss' house for that night, to which Bangwa readily agreed.

After sunset, Bangwa announced to his old maidservant that a guest was to join them for the evening and he would be spending the night with them. The old maid servant was not perplexed at this, for when once he had asked whether she can cook a delicious meal with chicken and tomato or not, the maid had boasted that there is not a single meal on earth that she cannot cook. This had once bewildered him, for how can a cook with limited access to the frivolous world outside and who had spent her entire life in a village near the stream do so. Wild chicken and roast potatoes were high on the menu, and Bangwa entertained his guest with a glass of cordial wine. But despite all this, the guest's attention was all fixed on the house. He was there to help and not for a weekend party. After finishing the wine and especially when the old maid had retired to the kitchen and the small adjoining room that was hers, Nkuyu got back to work. He had brought with him a small packet of white powder and dexterously sprinkled the same on the wooden floor that instantly produced a little smoke.

He looked at Bangwa who was watching all this with a bated breath. There was no doubt now that the house had been under the spell of black magic. The old maid was in the thick of cooking and Nkuyu told him that it would be good for them to find out the four nails that she had pierced deep in earth and that was holding the house from getting divine grace. This, as Nkuyu told Bangwa was also one of the reasons for his inordinate delay in getting married when he had been in favourable circumstances for over a year. An assured job in the upcoming rail project— what more could the bride's household expect? Nyuyu told him that they had to remove these nails pregnant with magic spells for the future course of action.

After the evening supper that was concluded rather quickly, Nkuyu came with a proposal. He had brought with him some charms that would be sufficient to cause the witch in the house fall asleep. Accordingly, when she was about to take a small nap (but would be vigilant enough in such moments), he sprinkled a small amount of red powder that caused sudden drowsiness in her. In moments, she was soundly sleeping, though only Nkuyu knew with what difficulty this had been accomplished.

Bangwa and Nkuyu went first to the end of the garden that harboured many small medicinal shrubs and other such trees. Here, Nkuyu again took out a small red ball with voodoo alphabets inscribed therein. He then dexterously rolled the ball in the north, then in the south and so forth. The ball instantly stopped in the corner of the garden that indicated that a nail was planted there. Nkuyu immediately took a shovel ans started digging the soft mud. Bangwa assisted him. After around one minute or so, a dark nail of around an inch presented itself. Three nails were yet to be traced.

Nyuku explained that the four nails that were planted in his courtyard were charmed and prevented any grace from entering the house. This he had easily understood when the powder he sprinkled exuded smoke. To cleanse the house they had to throw all of them into the flowing river. This would lessen the charm that haunted the house. Thus, without much further ado and delay, they started digging up all the four nails.

But something incredible happened when they were about to do so—when Bangwa had applied some force, he was immediately hurled back by some mysterious force. Nyuyu could very well understand that anyone who was not very well-versed in the tactics of voodoo would not be in a position to throw away the nails. Nkuyu had taken a lot of precaution to see to it that he could counteract the old maid's charms of black magic. To that end, he had smeared his hands with a protective layer of ash offered to the god of voodoo. So, he advised his host to stay away from the process of digging up the nails.

All the time the nails were being dug, the woman kept on murmuring strange voices from the hut. Perhaps she could see the destruction of her charm in her sleep but was rendered powerless to do anything due to the white magic employed by Nkuyu. Sometimes, the house shook a little, a scene that would render a non-believer a confirmed worshipper.

After around a hour had elapsed, it was time to throw away the nails into the flowing river nearby. Nkuyu then deliberated on what could be done with the witch. He could have killed her in sleep, but that would be sheer murder and the whites would be keen to implement their own set of laws on them. So, it was decided that she would be packed off to the temple of Obalata, the supreme Orisha or African God who was credited to have made the universe. It was only in that temple that her destructive powers could be cured and she be returned to docility.

Bangwa did what Nkuyu advised him to do. In the dead of night, she was brought to the temple where she was handed over to the arch-priest. It was told that he would supervise the next set of events.

Bangwa returned to his house by the break of dawn. He was relieved but the idea of missing a hearty, home-made lunch everyday rendered him depressed.'

Thus, I finished my tale. But by then, the old maid of seventy had probably listened to everything behind the curtains.

4. The Return

The last tale had its origins in dreams. So does this one.

One fine morning when me and my wife woke up, I could find myself as dirty as a corpse awaiting a wash before committed to the flames of daily routine. In fact, no one likes this Sisyphus-like punishment and philosophers have gone to lengths describing the human condition as such. I viewed myself in the mirror. My hair was disheveled, my eyes were grimy and my mouth exuded a foul smell that could have even driven away a smelly ram. Collecting myself like Mr. Bean of the animated series, I made for the washroom.

In the meantime, I offered my morning oblations and settled for breakfast. My wife was a bit crestfallen. She often is. The reasons are not hard to find. I still was far from getting a confirmed job; we were yet to have a new member in the family and my relationships with some of the people in my clan were not good. The last, however, is a universal phenomenon and I was not much perturbed about that.

I asked her the reason. She told me that its genesis lay in a dream that she dreamt the last night:

'The year is unspecified. So is the day. But my wife could well see that the house was this where we were having our breakfast. But it had been expanded to embrace the gate that sees a considerable portion of the same being left out to accommodate other activities. She told me that the outer portion had been expanded exactly in the same manner that the recent Municipality planner had told us to do. However, with this, the taxes would be high. Yet we went for it.

It is morning. The sun shines rather unkindly on the people around, and my wife tells me that she can see in her dream that she is tottering on the road, barely able to walk. She is around fifty then, her hair has been considerably clipped for reasons she cannot tell, and she somehow comes to the gate. The name of our house still sits rather snugly on the granite slab on which it had been inscribed before the same saw some major renovations before my marriage. The name had been kept in memory of my mother, but she had told me before dying that it should be kept in my name. Yet, we kept it in memory of the one who loved the house the most.

My wife cannot remember in what attire she was, but the sensation that she had after the dream told her that it was not presentable. She somehow reached the gates of the house. After the bell was rung, a fair boy of around sixteen came out. He was tall, like me around the eyes and the crown and had rather inquisitive eyes. "Whom to meet?" was the initial, natural query. Seeing her not answer but gaze all over, another girl of around fourteen came out. She did not resemble either my wife or me. She was not tall, rather plumb and had kind, expressive eyes. Her long hair reached near her waist and she was not very fair, but rather wheatish. But my wife stood watching them. After a good ten minutes had passed, a woman came out of the house. My wife could immediately understand that she was my second wife. She was fair, rather tall, had nice features and could be called beautiful. The boy had been exactly chiseled about her.

My wife told her about herself. Immediately, the trio got back to work. I was called from the office, but the attendant told me that I was busy in a meeting. The desperate message was sent that she had finally returned after eighteen long years. I came back in the evening as negotiating the jam of the city is no mean a task.

In the meantime, as my wife told me, she was escorted to the sitting room. The house no longer wore a desolate look, as it used to prior to my getting a confirmed job. Things that were redundant had been long removed, the sofas were new and the house had been brilliantly painted. My second wife got busy. My daughter made a wholesome meal for her and my wife was kind. In the evening, when I returned, I saw her finally. Her face had lost her former brilliance, but her eyes were still kindly. So, she had finally returned.

My wife further told me that the mishap from the waterfall that we visited eighteen years ago was to be blamed. We trekked some hills that were not far from our town; a train journey of around four hours was sufficient to get out of the hustle and bustle of the city. It was somewhere in September or October. Or the end of September and the beginning of October. The place was famous for its marble rocks and waterfalls. Falls that had medicated waters to cure you of asthma or other skin problems. Others never went near the turbulent waters and were more content in taking a snap here and there. People who did not get inside the water were often dubbed "unenterprising". My wife wanted to take a bath, but I resisted. But she had her reasons—you come so near to paradise and yet do not taste the nectar. But tasting the food of the Gods comes with its own, unique dangers. There were tourists and there were specialized men to take you to the middle of the waterfall; the "eye", as it was called there. It is only there that you could taste the "nectar". Despite my several warnings, my wife went for it. From the context of my wife's arrival, one can well comprehend what would have happened afterwards.

Sipping her tea, the next series of events were a fairy tale for all of us. After the man who was in charge of holding my wife's hand had slipped himself, the turbulent water fall took her away into the river within no time. She probably suffered a serious injury on her head. A search and rescue operation came to nothing. I was devastated.

After gaining consciousness, my wife found herself around six hundred kilometers away, in a village that specialized in manufacturing dye. There, she was to live a life by the munificence of an old man and a woman who had no children. They could quickly see that my wife had lost her memory and even after their best of efforts, she could not tell. Not even her name. Just a faint memory of water floated in her consciousness. The duo were kind enough to nurse my wife to health. Around ten years passed like this. Because of the conch shell bangles that my wife was wearing, it was difficult for them to marry off her again, though there were a good number of prospective men who had the desire to make her their bride. But the man and woman had a good say in the locality and such a thing never happened. After a good seventeen years had passed, she was once made to go near a waterfall to dry clothes. Such things now never took a toll on her health now . Many would persuade the old chaps to call the police and hand over her to them, but seeing my wife adamant not to go anywhere else (as she had taken them to be her own parents), they did not do such a thing.

Now after a good seventeen years, the clock had started to count backwards. It was the same river that was interspersed by waterfalls. Whenever she used to come near this water source, she could get a faint sensation of water running through her nostrils. The old woman (my wife had forgotten her name now!), would always persuade her to go there as that would help her regain her lost memories. And this is what happened that day. She had to venture deep into the eye of the waterfall and was carried again further deep into the river. But instead of drowning, she got it all over again—how seventeen years ago, she had gone deep into that selfsame waterfall and had lost all. She remembered her name, her house and all. The first thing to come into her head was her father's house. Immediately getting out of the water due to her superior swimming skills, she ran into a postman who told her that her native town was a good six hundred kilometers away. Acting sensibly, she sold her two gold earrings in a pawn shop and got some goodly sum of money. With some clothes and food, she boarded her bus for her hometown.

After around twelve hours, she landed on the soil that she had bid adieu years ago. Some of the houses were same, while others had changed. She could well see that time had quickly passed and that she was not the same woman. How were her parents? Her heart panted when she rang the bell of her house. It was a three story building now and well coloured.

A woman presented herself. "Whom do you want?"

"Where is my father, Mr. Shetty?"

The woman looked at her closely.

"Mr. Shetty is long dead. And Mrs. Shetty took to Haridwar some seventeen years ago. We bought this house then."

A thunderbolt landed on her then. Her whole world was in pieces. In the meantime, the long time neighbor of my wife's, Mrs. Durga came out. She instantly recognized her. She was dressed in widow's clothes, as her husband had died some years back. She wondered where on earth had she disappeared. My wife explained her.

Thus, after hearing all, she came to my wife, remembering the bus route very well.

She asked me why did I sell their house?

I told her that after her disappearance, it became increasingly difficult for me to manage both the houses. My father-in-law was distraught and my mother-in-law was increasingly losing her grip on reality. I used to visit them every alternate day. Then came the news of her father's death. My parents were also long dead. My mother-in-law decided to spent the rest of her time in a hermitage. It was difficult for me to manage both the properties. Thus, selling her house was the only option. After around four years had passed, my aunt told me to marry again, as I was still young. I was hesitant at first, but then, my new wife had met me at a mall and God knows how we developed a liking for each other.

 My wife listened. I was guilty of not having trusted she will return. We were silent.

When it was night, a strange sight presented itself to me. My second wife was talking with my wife with great interest, as if they were friends separated for a long time and my two children had also crept in to listen.'

After narrating this rather weird tale, my wife smiled. I was speechless.

5. To Let

Ramesh and his wife were fortunate enough to have a small, six hundred square feet flat in addition to their small house in the very heart of the city where you could virtually find everything except trust and love. Yet, there was enough bond between the couple, married for over six years. Ramesh had been working in a small enterprise as a contract executive that paid less, yet saw to it that he should turn up nice and trimmed by nine the next day. Yet, he persisted for around five years when all of a sudden, he was told to leave. No reasons. Just leave. Ramesh was handed his last month's cheque in a military fashion by the dusky personal assistant and an experience certificate. He came home and announced this to his wife. She had nothing to say. She was managing the home and that was an end to that.

In the evening, the couple set their mourning aside and decided to take stock of their situation on a war footing. Ramesh was teaching around five-six children, but then, their exams were due the next week. A dry period for another two months. Then, his wife had saved some ten thousand rupees and Ramesh's last pay (or pittance) would add to some nine thousand rupees more or so. No children till now. No, they were lucky not harbouring any concerns with an infant and the thousand things that are needed for a new-born. So, they had some to last for not more than two months. There was no guarantee that those six children after tuition should ever come back to him—depended on their performance in exams and what their mothers thought. Just that. The sanest choice in such an insane world like that was to let their flat. But then, you had to be careful. The Sangam complex near had seen a dozen court cases over a period of just three years, mostly dealing with the issue of eviction. Sometimes the tenants would just not pay in time. Then, in one weird case, a tenant had let his flat to yet another! The landlady was bewildered to see this and was rather coldly greeted by the proxy tenant who asked who she was. The landlady filed a case and the original tenant coldly answered that the contract never mentioned that a proxy tenant could be an impossibility. He would be paying his rent in time after all. The case continued for a well over five years and with a goodly damage to the lady.

Ramesh had heard such spine chilling tales about people who had let their flats. But then, you could be lucky—Mr. Ganjam who was the tenant of flat no. 6 of the complex in which he had his dwelling was a fine guy and the landlord never had any issues with him. "Fine deeds of previous life", Ramesh used to grin and report his wife.

The next task that Ramesh had to do was get in touch with some middlemen who used to part information with people who had their flats to let. But then, their hunger for the commission was great. He knew one such fella who would demand one month's full rent in lieu of giving a tenant to Ramesh. But then, you could not part with money when you have not made money. The tenant would be giving a security but then, that was meant to be returned at the time they would be leaving. The time the tenant was in, the middleman would be literally entering his bedroom for the money he has made. But thinking that would not help. He needed a tenant badly and that was it.

Then the middleman Shambu was there, Ratan was there and the list was endless. We went to Shambhu's house one day, and very soon got to learn that the whole family was in a nebulous situation. Shambhu had broken his mobile phone that he had just brought the last week. No reasons though. This had become a habit with him for some time now—a short tiff with his wife and his cell would be seen flying like a cruise missile through his small one bedroom house. But it was well-stocked with a fridge and a costly LED TV. "Good times, eh!", mused Ramesh. Seeing a prospective customer at the threshold of his house, he winked his wife to make some tea.

Ramesh straightforwardly came to the point and he was told that he would be seeing a gentlewoman the day next.

The morning sun cast its rays with great splendor, discriminating none and Ramesh was seen near his flat on the third floor. After a hour's waiting, three heads could be seen. One was apparently the man who wanted a dwelling on hire, the other was his wife (as he came to know later) and then the other was none other Shambhu. The man, after coming near, could be discerned middle-aged, anywhere between forty-five to fifty and quite proud of the way he carried himself. They were greeted warmly by Ramesh to which they answered with feeble replies. The man, with rat-like eyes was surveying Ramesh like a CIA agent or at least the one who would be marrying off his daughter soon. This made Ramesh a bit queasy.

After they had taken the lift and gone to the third floor, the man, a government detective by profession immediately started surveying the lift and asked how good was it. Ramesh replied that it had been newly installed and that the whole stuff was nicely done. He again asked what would happen to his ninety year old granny if the lift ever breaks down? To this, Ramesh replied patiently that the lift-breakdown team was ready to come to anyone's rescue within thirty minutes. But the man didn't seem convinced and after a quick look at the rather nice and comfy accommodation, began scrapping at the walls to see if the peel would come off or not. This invariably irritated Ramesh.

The next week, Shambhu presented himself with another would-be tenant. She had come alone and was looking for a flat with airy windows, and a balcony. But Ramesh's flat didn't have one, but the windows were large enough to let in a lot of air. But the woman, in her mid-thirties, was looking for a veranda that would give a nice view of the city, a purpose that was invariably served by the large, four feet by four feet windows. Then, she wanted the security to be down and the rent as well. To this end, Ramesh politely but firmly told her that perhaps his flat was not meant for her and that she was just wasting her time. He had a flat to rent and not a dream dwelling in Shangri-La!

This ordeal continued for some time. The money at hand was fast disappearing considering the price of foodstuffs that had escalated in the recent years. While the other flat owners in the complex were enjoying rent for quite some time and would soon get one when one had exited, the case was not the same with Ramesh and his wife. Around four months had passed and not a reliable soul in sight. Shambhu was just of the opinion that around a good dozen people had been benefitted by his services, Ramesh was the only exception. Ramesh was getting impatient. He had tried other brokers, but still, Shambhu was the only one who could give him some reliable information, a fact that the latter was very proud of.

Then, one fine afternoon, Shambhu presented himself on the door of Ramesh's household. He was given a rather warm welcome by his wife, who knew the tactics to make people work. After some tea, he came to the main task—a man wanted to see the flat. He lived in the city and was coming to see the flat on 'behalf' of his friend, a woman with two kids and two dogs. Ramesh was against keeping pets in the flat, but then, he had little alternative but to accept if the man, who was acting on behalf of his 'friend' liked the same.

After looking at the flat, the man liked it and conveyed over phone the lady in whom name the agreement was to be prepared. Upon asking where her husband was, the woman over the phone didn't say much. Yet, Ramesh agreed. The man handed him the xerox copies of the woman's identification papers for the agreement and told him that he would get the security within a day.

The sun shone with all its splendor on a June morning the next day. Ramesh got a phone from the man that announced that they were not in mood of moving into his flat and Shambhu would come late into the afternoon for the identification papers.

6. Buddhimaan

Arun's wife as well as Arun would be patiently waiting for "Buddhimaan" then, their two year old male pet cat who would have probably gone to have a walk outside before taking his nightly share of warm milk. What the couple feared was the group of ferocious dogs who may have ripped every part of his body, but Buddhimaan was so smart that he would come home unscathed. He had a sister in the house, a female cat called "Buddhu"—both were twins and their good mother had been just killed by a deranged dog a year back. The mother was nice, had kind eyes and would come to the household for some milk and a pat and would leave within some twenty minutes. After her sudden death, the two kittens were rendered defenseless and Arun and Asha had taken them into their charge. The couple still had no children and Buddhu and Buddhimaan would fill in their time. Buddhimaan had all the regard for his sister—when a bowl of milk was given to them in their 'teens', each would take alternate turns to sip the material. Budhu liked to hunt despite being given three meals a day, but Buddhimaan was timid and shy, would spend hours on the bed and would suddenly throw his head back against the wall and lean towards it after he had come home after a long stroll. "Could have been a Zamindar in his previous birth", Arun used to grin. Buddhimaan could not take the strain of an extended walk too much and would lie upside down like a sadhu or a baba doing yoga, with all his four legs upwards. Often, he used to wink with an eye to see if someone was watching him, or just to see if somebody had something to say regarding this attitude.

Then one day, Arun's father came in—he was living outside the town to his job that he still preferred to do after his retirement. One day, he had to use the washroom and just when he was about to enter, Buddhimaan was right there, responding to the call of nature by urinating at a safe spot. When this still continued well after a minute, Arun's father called him. Buddhimaan was still with himself and kept on looking at the ceiling wondering as if a CCTV camera had been installed or not to track his movements inside the washroom. Then, when around three minutes had passed, he silently walked down the room and settled, trying to recuperate after the heavy drainage of his bodily fluid. This would compel them to laugh.

Then, he had a queer habit of sitting on the window sill that would face the road from where all would enter the house. He would keep a strict eye on the gate and would wink whenever any body alien would pass. Could have been a dog in his previous life. Arun once took his photo with his smartphone and it is this one that he still, fondly keeps on staring even after Buddhimaan's death. He still cannot forget how Buddhimaan would insist sleeping with them and when the time to part with him and his sister would be ripe around twelve o' clock, Arun would take him away from his wife's lap and Buddhimaan, anticipating such an action from him would dig his sharp claws deep in the bed, insisting that he would stay. It would then be very difficult to wrest him out of his snug environs, but Arun would still be careful to catch both his paws lest he would get angry and slash through his face. But that never happened. After the door was closed, Buddhimaan and even his sister would join him in clanging the door stopper that would display their resentment and would continue till even one was not allowed inside. But the, there would be times when Arun and Asha would scream and the clanging would stop.

Buddhimaan was an exceedingly timid cat. Arun recalled fondly after his death how one day after work, when Asha was not around and the windows had been let open to let the duo in, the feline had been badly assaulted by a rival. This would be the case invariably—many stray cats would take every opportunity beat him and he would return home devastated. Once it happened that when Arun reached home, he called him, but after a good ten minutes, Buddhimaan was nowhere to be found. Then upon checking under the bed, there was he! Extremely petrified, his tail had been nearly severed by a malignant bite from that rival cat and the untidy and creased bed linen showed that he had been badly ravaged while fighting with the goon. Arun somehow coaxed him into the assurance that no cat was around and that he could safely come out. Buddhimaan did. When Asha arrived, she was nearly dead to see his favourite pet in such a miserable condition. She immediately washed his wound and used a costly ointment to nurse his flashy tail. It was only after a month's nursing that he was well.

Then suddenly, after around a year or so, Buddhu was pregnant and had delivered three cute kittens. But keeping them in the house would have increased the population, so upon much deliberation over the matter, Asha told Arun to deliver the kittens to a nearby house that kept pets as such. That somehow save them from the vagaries of the world and there was a good chance that they may well find a home. But the reach catch was Buddhu herself—if the kids were taken in her presence, there was a good chance that she would not mind ripping off either Arun's or Asha's arm. So the deed was done in Buddhu's absence. When she returned, there was a curious look in her eyes. But then, nothing happened after that.

Then one fine evening, Buddhu came home, but was shaking badly. Asha could well understand that it was a case of blood poisoning that was often accompanied by failed conception and particularly when the fetus had failed to detach from the body. She was shaking horribly and then, after a minute or so, the shaking would stop, only to resume again. This agony continued well all over the night. Asha kept on weeping and Arun could not but help ringing a veterinary surgeon, only to be replied that he checked patients in the clinic and that home call was not possible. Buddhu's agony went past a phase and in the wee hours of the morning, she was dead. Buddhimaan was kept locked up in the bedroom lest he should see the degrading circumstances into which Buddhu had fallen. When Buddhimaan could hear Buddhu's screams, he would just in the direction from where the noise had floated. But then, all could not be prevented—when Asha was persuaded by Arun to go to sleep and leave her as nothing could now be done. When it was morn, Buddhimaan sneaked out of the small gap in the door that had not been totally shut to see what was going on. Buddhu had already died by then and Asha's grief knew no bounds. Buddhimaan kept on circling around his sister. It was evident that he had been badly shaken. Buddhu was taken to the local crematorium where there was a little patch cleared for dogs and cats and infants who had died. Animals are not usually buried with any well-known rites, but Buddhu had the privilege of a red cloth, a deep grave, flowers, incense, intense tears and a coin for the mythical ferrycat who may await her in the feline underworld.

After Buddhu's death, Budhimaan was not debarred from sleeping on the bed that Arun and Asha shared. In the midnight, Arun would look up at him and would see Buddhimaan with his eyes fixed at a particular direction. He would be inevitably searching his sister, and Arun would sometimes take him in his arms and press his face deep into his and would notice the slow breathing of the estranged creature. He was slowing dying and Asha was told that the day would soon come. Budhimaan could not think of the world without his cute sister—Arun had noticed that both of them would even go to the limit of playing the cop and the thief game. Buddhu would suddenly come into a room and hide behind the door. Then would Buddhimaan come, unaware that she was lurking behind. Then, with a leap that reminds one of martial arts movies, she would catch him unawares. Arun would laugh during such moments as he had very little idea that cats too played such games.

With such a bond severed, Buddhimaan would spend hours outside home. He was inevitably searching for her. Then, one afternoon, when it was lunchtime, Buddhimaan had not come to take his due morsel. Asha was worried because of the dogs. After it was around five, she decided to inspect. After going a good hundred yards, she enquired an old lady who told her that a young cat, very healthy and white, had come to their courtyard and had died after an hour. Her grandson had thrown the body near the field that was full of shrubs. Asha knew this was it. She asked the gentle lady to show her the way. In the meantime, Arun had come and he kept on telling her that there were around sixty stray as well as domestic cats in the neighborhood and that the cat that was described dead may not be him. But Arun knew inside that Buddhimaan was no more.

The duo crossed the brambles and then a body was visible. Upon inspection, it was him. A thunderbolt had landed on the couple. Buddhimaan had probably died of a heart failure as there were no visible marks on his body to prove the existence of a dog attack. His body had been rendered cold, his flashy tail was stiff. He had been dead over eight hours.

Buddhimaan was given the same funerary rites as her sister. He was laid in a deep grave beside her, in whose memory he had refused to live.

7. The Pyramid Builder

Rajan was an international expert in Egyptology and had spent over ten years in the study of the hieroglyphics. His publications were mostly concerned with the manner in which this enigmatic script that flourished over 4,000 years ago had changed over a period of time. His research work had convinced him that the ancient Egyptians used two kinds of scripts—one that was used in day-to-day record-keeping and one that was used exclusively for the embalming process. The latter was infinitely more complex. Another fancy that had just caught his attention was the probable discovery of a scroll in Luxor that may give the world some inkling of how the great pyramid of Giza of Khufu was built. For years, Egyptologists had racked brains as regards the actual process that may have been used—some suggested that an external ramp, as long as 1.5 kms. was laid and the sandstone blocks were hauled up. Then, some queer sci-fi, self-made specialists would argue that a mammoth work on such a scale was actually engineered by the extraterrestrials. "Bah!" Rajan would baulk. The edifice was the result of sheer muscle power, this he was sure of. But who were the actual people who built the only structure that remained the world's tallest till the Industrial Revolution came in? What went on in their primitive minds when they worked? Their hopes, joys and aspirations?

After around a week's hard labor with his Egyptian assistant El-Haroon Makd, Rajan came across a queer scroll. It was in fair condition and had been found near the small tomb of a pyramid builder who had, in all probability, volunteered the pyramid of Khafra. "Ok. Not Khufu but his son's!" Rajan exclaimed. The pyramid of Khafra was just a little short of Khufu's. Back in his tent, he slowly started to decipher what happened 4,300 years ago. The narrative was recorded by a highly skilled mason called "Kumtpethph", an unusual name for a worker. It went on like this:

'The pyramid of Khufu, whose excellent White Crown submits all to His will, is complete. Khafra wants a similar structure, but Khufu's pyramid has rendered Egypt bankrupt; the Nile has watered as much as she could. There are conspiracies in the royal court to remove Khufu and place him untimely in the tomb that he has so lavishly built for himself. The population that built the Great Pyramid is old and decrepit now—after twenty years of hard labor, their old bones have nothing much to offer. The casualties are over 2,000 men who died building and over 6,000 who were injured. I was just seven years old when the pyramid had started, and am twenty eight now. My father, who participated for over five years as a free man said that there was someone breaking his bones after every 6 hours. Yet, the best of physicians were dispatched every time such an incident occurred. Yet Khufu has been a good king and his reign has seen no major rebellions. The Syrian chieftains wanted to overrun our sacred land seeing the economic mess all around, but Khufu had kept the medjai [2]well fed from a contingency fund that was kept in good condition since the time of the Second

Dynasty. Yet, Khafra, our prince wants a similar structure. He will be a living God when he ascends the throne—the son of Amun Ra [3] and the High Priest of every temple in Egypt.

Khufu is over seventy now and does not want to alienate his good son. So, just three years after the labour force had barely rested when Khufu's royal announcers one day came to my village. There was an announcement that around 20,000 able bodied men would be needed and daughters over 11 should also report. I could well understand that my role would be that of an overseer, as I was rather lanky and would be more comfortable with mathematical calculations. A greater reward was announced—people whose taxes were due need not pay any after assured work on this second structure after 5 years, while provisions for each man slaving everyday would be two huge breads for lunch, two solid pieces of meat, two duck eggs, a bunch of grapes and abundant water. Plus a bath in cool waters after seven hours of non-stop work. Total hours would not exceed ten, and there would be a night shift, as they had in Khufu's time. But the dangers of the work would be great. I may be asked to have a look at the quality of limestone blocks from Aswan and measure them with the assistance of others in the searing heat of the Sahara.

So, the next morning, I was told to take farewell of my wife and my little child who still ran naked even after having started going to his teacher. We are not rich, but my wife is fortunate enough to have a maid, Ntemp, who is now our greatest help in most of the matters. She would fetch water from the Nile and wash our clothes, yet my wife would not leave cooking to her. My father cautioned me to take frequent breaks for, being an overseer, I could. The royal men from the court had come to take me—I was handed over a stole that read "one of the royal overseers" that had the picture of Osiris [4] on it. With two huge insignia bearing the figures of the crocodile god Sobek and the holy serpent Uraeus, I quickly walked away. My father had earned a good record and I was reaping the fruits.

The site already had been chosen. It was meant to be built next to Khufu's. The area had been selected by the Chief Priest, Hamuntereptu. He had consecrated the land with holy ash and Khafra had been proclaimed the next son of Amun-Ra. Khufu had already made the declaration that he would be the next mortal God of Egypt. But that meant only one thing—the mega structure had to be completed before he died or plague and darkness would descend upon Egypt and eat the land. Most of the labourers were busy chiseling lime stones and were already in the thick of the job. I was told to oversee a portion that would later see a ramp made of rubble and dirt going up the pyramid. As the ramp was yet to rise, I was supposed to observe and check the degree of inclination that the capstone would need to reach the top. Khafra had ordered that his pyramid should be a goodly 136 meters high and as he had a great respect for his father, the same ought not be equal to his father's structure. The day I joined the work, the base of the pyramid had already been constructed. The main issue for the labourers was a stone block, weighing over 50 tonnes, that was to be hauled. We used over 200 men and a lot of mud from the Nile to loosen the sand that had been an impediment for the smooth movement of the limestone blocks. After a good seven hours, the mammoth task was finished. The workers were given a compulsory rest of around an hour and a bath in the Nile. The lower priest under me was supposed to recite charms for them so that the God Sobek would save them from the crocodiles in the waters.

After this had continued for over a week, I went to my house as I could not visit due to the strain of the work and my compulsory attendance for the first week. At noon, when I reached my house on the eastern bank of the Nile, my wife could be heard talking with a man whom I did not know. When she saw me, she introduced him to be her old friend's husband who had come to our house to invite us for a feast in the honour of their daughter who was pregnant after a long time. She had been married for around six years now and, at last, been blessed with a baby. The man was easy with my wife and upon asking, told me that he was a wine trader and an occasional fruit merchant. He wore good clothes, a leather boot (only worn by the rich) and not those lowly, made of reeds and a long chain of glass jewellery. He had rather sly eyes and a long nose like that of a parakeet. I humbly told him that I would not be able to go to the feast due to my engagement at the pyramid building site. He didn't say anything to that. It became evident after he had gone that he had managed to leave a good impression on my wife.

Even after the feast was over, there were times when he would come to our house. I asked my father regarding this and he replied that he was too old to understand the ways of the youth, though I was approaching thirty-five and surely not a 'youth', my father was seventy. Then, one evening, my wife and I had a good quarrel over this. She was just brushing her hair with a new comb made of ivory that had replaced the wooden that she used. I asked her regarding this.

"Djwardeft gave me", she replied casually.

"And what happened to those that you used?"

She didn't answer.

I grabbed her fiercely. She resisted and told me that she had thrown them! That was nearly blasphemy. In Egypt, a woman could not throw a comb without the presence of the man who gave them. If he was dead, you had to summon one of the relatives from his side. She had paid no heed to such customs. This meant only one thing. The break in conjugal relationship, especially if the woman had used them for more than five years.

I asked again, "What happened to my combs?"

She was a bit shaken. "I threw them."

I felt like grabbing her throat and strangling, but I loved her. She was still holding her ivory combs that the outsider had given her. My eyes were set on those. I wanted to break them, but good sense that prevailed told me not to do that. But I could well see that she had thrown them deliberately.

After a week's work on the quarry and the intricate measurements that I completed, I decided to probe the matter and discuss the same with a fortune teller. He was a very old man who sat outside the walls of the Temple of

Horus at Edufu. Even the Vizier had once come to meet him. He was called "Nannir", a Mesopotamian name. He probably was half-Egyptian, half Mesopotamian by birth and it was said that he could tell things by the subtle use of magic that was a cross breed between both these great civilizations.

I met him in the evening. He was relieved after the cool air from the Sahara had fanned him after the day's heat. I told him that my wife had secretly chosen someone else after around seven years of marriage. He asked me if I had a lame son to which I answered in the affirmative. He produced a femur bone and sprinkled some white powder to it and also applied the same on my forehead. That gave a cool sensation to my body, but I was nearly petrified to see that the bone had started to exude smoke. Then he said that my wife would ask for a divorce under the testament of Ptah, the arch creator God on the pretext that I could not help her produce a healthy offspring and that she should be allowed to leave me. When I asked if we could go ahead for yet another, he smiled and said that my wife would not allow that. It was a bit late. As a remedy, he gave me an amulet that I had to wear on my arm and that would probably bring in the change within her.

Back home, I had my food and in the night, under the great stars of Nut [5] I fell asleep. This invariably happened whenever I came home from the quarry. And this damned pyramid would be the tomb of my conjugal relationships as well. I had no time for my home now, this had been steadily going for the last two years and my wife was bound to find affection somewhere else. But that she would go to the ridiculous limits of throwing away the comb was what gave me sleepless nights.

One day, a man broke his arm while lifting a block of stone with others via a pulley. Immediately, the royal physician was dispatched for much-needed medical attention. Since one man was short for the proper setting of the block, I too had to help. But when the block had reached the cubicle, my amulet was badly crushed by the edge of a stone. It was broken into two halves. And that meant only one thing. Disaster. Sheer disaster!

A day after the incident, I was told not to come to the site for a week as I had earned sufficient leave to warrant so. A new man was appointed, a brat who had no idea of pyramid block measurements. The pyramid of Khafra was taking shape, but far from the day of the final, golden capstone being set and the consecration by the High Priest who had his headquarters in the Temple of Karnak.

The evening next, I went to the fortune teller gain. He could not give me a second amulet, for he told me that it would be useless.

Matters were slipping away from my hands as months passed with the annual flooding of Nile. The fortune teller had nearly given me an inkling that since the consecrated amulet was lost, it meant only doom. I awaited with a bated breath what was to come next. After years of our relationship, my wife presented me with a letter that asked for the annulment of our marriage! It had the sanction of the Vizier and the law of Isis that stipulated that if the first child was born a lame and if no child was fathered within four years of the birth of the lame child, then the marriage was deemed cancelled. The wife would have the right to inherit half the property of the husband. I could well see the wily intentions of that bitch whom I had loved. I immediately took the scroll and left for the second most powerful man in the whole of the land of the Nile, the Vizier, Seutempateftsu who had his office in the temple of Karnak.

But visiting the Vizier was just like having the privilege of paying a visit to the God Amun-Ra Himself, the King of Gods . I asked the lower medjai that it was a matter of my life, but they wouldn't allow me. They laughed. When I told one that I was assigned a high post as a pyramid builder, they were not bothered as well. They told me that such "high posts" were as ephemeral as the sand dunes near the Nile, and after one had fallen sick, another would come. After waiting a long time, I had to return knowing well that it was a heavy purse from my wife's lover that had allowed her in.

My wife got the divorce within six months and moved with her paramour. My father said nothing, as he had already been wasted considerably and had always decided not to interfere with our private matters. However, after about a month, he asked me if I could have helped it. I said that I couldn't, and even if I could, I would have told her to leave anyway. There was no need for a woman who had violated the norms of marriage. My father breathed his last three months later and was accorded a grand funeral from the royal treasury for being an ardent servant in service of Khufu and having solved many intricacies of pyramid building. He was the "Niet Shre Sat Abusbe Osshs" now: the builder of builders and the most efficient mason, worthy to be ranked among such master builders like Imhotep, that excellent man who worked under the Great Pharaoh Djoser, now deified by us all. He was accorded a costly mummification.

On the horizon shone the golden capstone of Khafra's pyramid one fine morning, after twelve more years. Our living God had been assured eternity forever, when, leaving the mortal body, He would join the company of Gods and look over Egypt, tending both the lucky and the luckless alike.'

Rajan closed the scroll. He had apparently decided to publish it, but he would not now. He had decided not to divulge a tale of greed, helplessness and faithlessness that had unfolded around 4,300 years ago in the ancient world.

8. The Ten Rupee Note

Many look at me with askance when a rickshaw driver or a vegetable vendor gives me as a change to a customer. The initial reactions are those of doubt—whether I am torn or not to that of fear of contamination if the same comes from a fish market or a butcher shop. Most of the times, I am dirty, being one of the most common of currency denominations in the Indian subcontinent. But on certain occasions, I am neat and trim as a groom who has, after all, found his bride after years of waiting. Well, emotions differ; you never know what simmers in the head of people whom God has doled out of his heavenly factory. All I can remember is that I am well over fifteen years old, very dirty and looking for deliverance soon. But the day when I was churned out of the factory is something I cannot well remember. What I can is a day when an unemployed man had me in his kind pocket. He was not a miser, but was compelled to, owing to the excellent recruitment systems in our nation. He was determined to save me for buying a present for his lame sister who had just been operated. Yet, in the rush hour in the streets, I fell. He kept searching me for over an hour, but no luck. I was compelled to become grimy, as it was monsoon and no sooner had I fallen than I was rescued by a beggar who had just bought a television after twenty years of begging. What I came to know was his wife begged as well, though she was not accomplished in this fine art and lacked the much needed niceties in her begging arsenal.

The moment the beggar got me, he was determined to buy something for his wife. His wife may have been a miser, having made her mind to save every penny, as she had just ventured into this business and invested into a mat and a shiny begging bowl and had to pay a monthly sum of a hundred rupees to the street inspector who belonged to the municipality. Hence, a ten rupee slipping from her hands was a veritable catastrophe. But the husband had been into this for over twenty years and decided to buy some snacks for his wife for the evening. He had made it clear the last night that he would be maintaining his own separate account in the post office savings bank—this had infuriated his wife to a great extent. Since she loved samosas, he bought two and both had a nice time, as I still believe.

The man with the snacks looked at me and after inspecting every fiber of my body, kept me near the frying pan. I endured this agony for over five days. Each time something would be thrown into the scalding oil, some drops would fall on me and I would gather more grime. The second day, a man was supposed to get ten rupees back; the man handed over me to the customer, but the latter refused after inspecting the grime and muck. He looked like a rice merchant and the way he summarily rejected me was as if he would reject a prospective bride for his son. He narrowed his eyes, his nostrils were disfigured and with a hand that brushed me off, I was again in the snacks shop. The deliverance came only ten days later when a man in hurry did not care to inspect me from head to toe.

I changed hands but the moment the office goer put me in his breast pocket, I was overcome with nausea. He had landed into an overcrowded bus and was in hurry. He kept on calling people, telling them he was on his way. The month of June added to my woes. I was totally covered with sweat and had he not put his entire wad of cash on the desk under the fan, I may well have broken into two pieces. The moment was indeed exhilarating—I was laid with the notes of other denominations, higher than me who were well trimmed as well. The five hundred rupee note looked at me as if he were asking if I would need a job and the twenty rupee took her face away. This game of subordination endured well for over five hours when I was ready to go home.

The man probably lived very far from his office and had to take a suburban train to commute. But the way he took yet another ticket that was probably not his destination made me smell a rat. Come on, I am just a currency and not fit to speak about people's affairs, but the man just got off the train and hurriedly turned into a dinghy area that was peopled with men and women who cannot be called to belong to any respectable part of the town. He was received by a woman who coquettishly looked at him, and her body language showed that he was a regular. That was a shock! I went inside as well and after around an hour or so, he was off.

Back home, his dutiful wife greeted him and asked why he was late today. The man twitched his brows and then told her that the daily train that he took had developed some snags on the way that left him stranded with thousands. I was taken aghast at this lie. From this time onwards, I prayed to my creator that I would not stay in that accursed man's pocket for even a minute, but certainly I had no wings to zoom somewhere else. I remained in his shirt for a week more when he went to the pawnbroker's shop to get an antique item back that he had pawned to get some money for the girl whom he worshipped outside his home. I was glad that I had escaped that man's reach. May God be with his wife.

The pawnbroker was a burly man, wearing around a good twenty grams of gold chains on his neck; his fat fingers were equally adorned with five gold and one platinum ring. He was very sure about his business and the place where he kept me was neat and clean as a temple or any other place of worship would be. At first, my reactions ranged from those of mirth, exhilaration and even bordered on feelings of nirvana one would get after years of hardship. But then, the hard fact landed straight on my face. The man was also involved in the printing of counterfeit notes that were smuggled all over the nation and that had its base outside the country. This I came to know when a guy with smart looks, chewing a costly cigar and with a sunglass came to him one fine evening. There were customers still milling around in his shop that kept nearly everything from antique statues to diamond rings. The pawnbroker immediately took him to the room where he kept his cash box that harbored me as well. From their conversations, I came to know that a new consignment of fake notes were about to come from across the border and that he had well paid the police personnel in advance deployed over there. After that, the discussions switched over to the grand party that was to be thrown in honor of the "boss" who was to arrive that night, coupled with the fact that a belly dancer girl had been specially ordered who was known for her killer smiles and feminine charms. May God save me from such scenes, I am an old chap now, keeping with the standard fact that a note like me often is deemed senile after seven years of heavy use. The boss arrived, and by the time the dancer girl had come, I was snoring. A matter of advanced years. The next day, when the pujari had come to pay obeisance to the idol in his shop and did his normal tasks, I was off with the priest.

And this continued for over nine months—I was travelling a lot and was everywhere. In shopping malls, in the vanity bags of well perfumed belles, in the railway reservation counter hearing the incessant chatter of people that the government had been cruel in hiking rail fares and in a college fees counter where a student deposited me with much difficulty. He was working part time in a pizza shop and after having worked over eleven hours a day for three months, had succeeded in depositing his one-time college fees for the diploma in management degree that he had been dreaming of for quite some time to pursue. His father was a chowkidaar in a house of a well-to-do man who saw to it that he be paid less. Yet, human endeavors win and he deposited me along with notes of other denominations to the head clerk of a college that admitted him finally. I was tired to the bone and settled for a siesta.

When I awoke, it was nine o' clock in the morning. It seems that I had overslept. The head clerk had received his monthly salary and he was giving it to his wife, a woman with a kindly face. She was thoroughly inspecting each and every note when I landed in her face. She was infuriated how he could have accepted a nearly damaged currency! The man took me near to his face, examined and told her that since nothing could be done now, he would keep me in his house, near the currency box with a gesture of good will as the northern part of the cupboard should never be empty.

And when I looked at the man, I could see that he was the same unemployed guy who had lost me that fateful day on the road. So after around two years of sojourn, I had finally found a home.

With a sigh of intense relief, I let my eyelids fall.

9. A Day In The Life Of A Suburban

He would be careful to wind his clock to seven in the morning and when it would ring, somehow adjust himself and lead towards the bathroom. Looking himself into the mirror, he would first examine his face and see if he at all needed a shave. If it was imminent, the razor would be examined for its sharpness and the arduous process would begin within five minutes. He would not spend more than fifteen minutes on ablutions as missing the nine fifteen local would be a complete disaster, especially when you're working on a contractual basis. He thought much about this in the past but now, he didn't. In the meantime, he would hear his wife rise from the bed, settling her long hair into a bun, who would be quick to prepare tea. He would have finished by shaving by now and sporting a white dhoti that was once bought from a south Indian temple, would settle for the puja. The sanctum would be adorned with almost all the Hindu gods worshipped and he would be careful with the hymns. A clock had been installed there as well to tell him the passage of time. A Medieval knight chasing the Holy Grail. Then, after all was over, he would have his tea, wear his clothes in a military fashion and would be gone. With the wind. Taking an auto would mean struggling with many near the bus stop, but with a speed that would put our Spiderman to shame, he would nevertheless catch one. In the auto, his tie would keep on flying as if it were a signal from a speeding train bent on wreaking havoc. Once, it would have got itself entangled with the horns of a bull while the auto was passing through a narrow lane, but Lord Shiva somehow instructed his mount to spare him. And he was.

He would invariably have a short 'lunch' in the restaurant that served meals to office goers in the morning. The Tripti Restaurant, established in 1921, was well-equipped with staff that prepared food and kept everything ready, as people like him would not brook any delay. On seeing him rushing to the shop, the old man in charge of the morning shift would instantly start preparing the vessel—steaming rice, dal, onions, a slice of lemon, a side curry of seasonal vegetables and fish or eggs as he desired. He would prefer eggs, as fish would require the elaborate ritual of taking away the thorns. That was also one of the ways to keep the bill low to around fifty rupees. The egg would be consumed carefully with small bites lest the entire stuff be over and the remaining meal would still await something delicious. Extra vegetable side dish would be free only for twice. After this, he would rush to the railway station with just five minutes remaining for the train, as he always kept season tickets with him to avoid the long queue of purchasing a daily ticket. That was also a sane way to keep the commuting charges low as well.

The interior of the local train would be pure hell with people having descended from every part of the planet. You would find office-goers, lawyers, brokers, pimps and what not sharing the same car. He would not wait for the train to come to a complete halt and would catch the handrail that acted as a support to install his presence there. The would be great, like a Mumbai suburban local, if not more and by the time the train had already left the platform, many would still be hanging. But being of a slim constitution, he would manage to get in. Then he would take out an S-shaped iron rod from his bag and hang the handle into it and suspend from the iron net. Since only faces are visible during those times, once, when he had taken out the improvised structure, someone took him to be a butcher going to the slaughterhouse. He shouted at him to maintain distance and he still remained quiet. He had gathered a crude impression that since the hook was used to hang mutton generally, our office goer was all set to murder some more goats. But he remained mute still. Our hero does not talk much now-a-days, and with very good reasons.

After being in that hell hole for around forty minutes, our hero lands on the main terminus station today as well. He is besmeared with sweat and some flowers that a woman had accidently dropped on the crowd in his home station. With no time to loose and already a bit late, he joins the milling crowd that descends down the enormous staircase. When he often looks back, only heads are visible. "Count the heads", he remembers the phrase. The journey in the bus would be equally tedious as well, though there were air conditioned buses, the fares would be high. By the time he reaches the office, he would be already half-dead due to exhaustion.

He was working as a front office keeper in an IT company that had been recurring losses each year. They would be changing people after every four months and hiring 'new talent' and promising them everything. Like leaders during elections. Our hero had just joined a month back after having sitting idle for over five months. He was supported by a flat that had been let but then, just six thousand bucks do not keep the body and soul together in a megacity! So, back-breaking work in the office and attending every foolish call with the polite words "How may I help you?" That used to get on his nerves and by the time it would be around three, he would be ravenously hungry again. Then, it would be the time to take out a cup cake from his bag and eat the same with some tea that would be delivered by the office boy. Some of the files would be presented to him that had to be compulsorily cleared by the end of the day. Once it happened that a file was still pending clearance and he could only reach home by ten. He remembered that still and saw to it that no file remained on his desk by five pm.

When he was in thick of work, the IT manager came and asked him how was all going. He rose and greeted him as he was the son-in-law of the boss who had the nasty habit of removing employees every four months and bringing in new with lesser wages. The manager inspected some files and was not happy with the way the entire stuff was proceeding. He told him that he was no longer to be entrusted with the job and that a new chap was to take his charge by the end of the day. Our warrior does not ask anything, as asking would not help. And he was not in a mood to risk his job and the little money that was coming from there. Like a cop on duty saluting a leader, he agreed. By two, a shiny, macho guy arrived. Some gossips revealed that he was a distant relative of the IT manager who used to lie idle in his house like cow dung that no one liked to lift and make it into a veritable source of fuel. He was about six feet, very muscular, may have been a part-time model on some obscure ramps around the city, wore diamond rings in his four fingers, was well groomed and arrived jubilantly as if he had solved the problem of black money in India. "Hi everybody!" were the first words that he announced. A lady receptionist winked at him and pursed her lips. He came near to our hero and asked him what he was supposed to do. He handed all the files to him and told him that the data therein had to be operated in the machine. At this, the guy looked weakly as if he had contacted measles. He immediately left the table and headed for the office of the manager. After a few minutes, the manager came and told him that he was to remain where he was, as he was "unfired".

When it was around quarter to five, the Boss came and told everyone that due to an urgent meeting that was to take place the next day, they all had to labor more till seven. The model had left by then. He had to. Our hero called his wife that he would not be home till nine thirty. His was dizzy with work and then those two hours looked like as millennia to him. However, time and girlfriends wait for none and by the time it was seven, he was gasping for breath, much like others.

He took the eight-fifty local train that was again peopled with all imaginable sections from this planet. In the crowd, he somehow managed a seat. The man opposite to him was reading a newspaper that said that a government official had been seen begging to raise money for his father's funeral rites. Another said that a jewellery shop had not been looted despite the lock being broken, only the sofa sets were missing. He was tired to the bone. A man was selling masala puffed rice and he ordered one. That was good.

At home, his wife was waiting as usual. The tea was already cold. He looked at his face in the mirror after a full ten hours.

Another day had passed....

10. We Got Works To Do

Tarun had a huge issue waking up early, coupled with the fact that he had to be on time in the departmental store's godown when the week's consignment arrived. He had been working for the last six months only and the task of looking into the huge packets of clothes got on his nerves. He was thoroughly exhausted when he went home. At forty, he was still a bachelor and with both his parents dead was alone on this planet. Of course he had his share of uncles and aunts but then they never really bothered to call him on weekdays. So, Tarun did not really care. After all, what's the use of such people, he would sometimes think. His life was as flat as a cricket pitch where even the deftest spinner would be futile with his share of tactics. So, nothing really changed. He lazed till seven in the evening after he had gone home by five and the rest of the time would be spent buying some veggies and meat in the evening bazaar and cooking his own meals. He would do this with the TV still on till one at night. And when he would awake with nothing to motivate him in the morning, he would murmur "we got works to do!" and be instantly out of bed as if he had been stung by a wasp.

And the day would begin.

Of course, there were people who would tell him to get married, but then, living in a one bedroom house with the toilet outside would not invite any prospective man to give his daughter's hand in marriage. Plus he had no confirmed job and just slaved day and night in the godown that just gave him enough to keep the body and soul together. He was tall, around six feet and fair, but not with the resources to start a family. His father had saved some but then most of that had been consumed with his mother's disease that left them financially crippled. He was working in the store for the last five years and had saved some in the post office and in a cooperative bank. Approaching forty, it would be difficult for him to do things in a smooth manner as he had done had he been in his prime. He still was, but then opportunities slipped and destiny never smiled upon him. Just a life and nothing to count on. And the refrain "we got works to do" was all that carried him forward, for, without his routine he was a cripple. And it was just his daily routine that carried him forward. That maintained his level of sanity.

However, he was not without the niceties of youth. One day, while going to his damned shop, he saw a belle and it was the latter who had been eyeing him for quite some time. She was of a medium built and had a long hair that was tied as a bun. She did not wear any jewelry but had kajal around her eyes and sported earrings. And then, just within a span of a month, they were in a coffee shop.

"We have been meeting for a month now", said Srijita.

"Yes. You got problems with that?" Tarun grinned.

"No, but what next?", Srijita was serious.

Tarun could very well discern that she was contemplating marriage. She was silent.

"Father wants to meet you!"

Tarun did not answer.

"What do you say?"

"I shall meet him as well."

Srijita knew very well that Tarun did not have a steady-going income. But she was working as a school teacher and the job was to be confirmed very soon. She wanted Tarun to tell her father that he worked in a company, but Tarun did not desire to build a relationship on a heap of lies.

"I will support you when we marry. We will manage."

"My godown does not pay me enough, but with the new manager coming in, maybe, things would be better."

After around a week, Tarun went to meet Srijita's father. The man was a kind guy but not without common sense that would help one steer in this real world. He listened to Tarun and after inspecting everything, decided to meet the manager of the godown in which he worked to know what Tarun indeed got. Was it just a measly sum of eight thousand rupees or even less? Otherwise, the man liked Tarun and had inwardly decided to marry off his only child with him.

The next day, Srijita's father went to the office of the new manager of the store who informed him that they had fired Tarun in the morning and that a new guy was to step in his shoes from that evening.

Around a week later, Tarun woke rather early. He had somehow managed to join as a waiter in a restaurant that warranted that he work till ten at night and be there again at nine in the morning. And Tarun's ears gave him the selfsame message "we got works to do". He had to hurry as it was his first day, which could well be his last.

Appendix

Also by the same author:
Poetry
In Desolate Dwellings
Residence Beneath the Earth
The Wind in the Abyss
The Golden Harvest
September Songs
Penitent Night: A Book of Haiku Poetry
A Violent Spring & Other Poems
Guernica
Footnotes of History: A Tale of the Mahabharata
Cranberry Heart
Drama
A Meeting & Other Plays
Hamlet ay 220/G & Other Plays (forthcoming)
Fiction
P.: A Novel

Notes

1. A derogatory term for the British stationed in India during the British Raj.

2. The royal body guards of the Pharaoh.

3. A fusion of two gods, namely Amun, the creator of the universe, and Ra or Re, the sun god, he was one of the major gods in the Egyptian pantheon and considered a supreme deity by the 5th dynasty in ancient Egypt.

4. The god of the underworld, fertility and resurrection in Egyptian mythology and a major deity.

5. The sky goddess in ancient Egypt.